MW00989222

BUTTERFLY

Colour By Number

By Sachin Sachdeva

Other books by **Sachin Sachdeva**

"Colour By Number" Series

Easter
Sea Life
Mandala
Mermaid
Christmas
Halloween
Doll House
Love Treats
Sugar Skulls
Trick or Treat
Happy Halloween
Flowers & Butterflies
A Day at the Circus
St. Patrick's Day
Cute Animals
Dress Up
Butterfly
Magical
Vehicles
Pirates
Birds

Available on Amazon.com

Copyright 2021, Sachin Sachdeva

All rights reserved. No part of this book may be reproduced or used in any way or form or by any means whether electronic or mechanical, this means that you cannot record or photocopy any material ideas or tips that are provided in the book.

This book belongs to

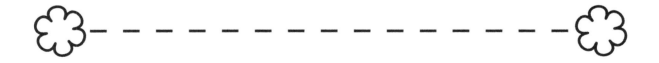

1= Yellow   2=Brown   3=Blue   4= Green

5=Pink   6=Purple   7=Red

1= Yellow   2=Brown   3=Blue   4= Green

5=Pink   6=Purple   7=Red

1= Yellow   2=Brown   3=Blue   4= Green
5=Pink   6=Purple   7=Red   8=Orange

1= Yellow   2=Brown   3=Blue   4= Green
5=Pink   6=Purple   7=Red   8=Orange

1= Yellow   2=Brown   3=Blue   4= Green

5=Pink   6=Purple   7=Red   8=Orange

1= Yellow   2=Brown   3=Blue   4= Green
5=Pink   6=Purple   7=Red   8=Orange

| 1= Yellow | 2=Brown | 3=Blue | 4= Green |
| 5=Pink | 6=Purple | 7=Red | 8=Orange |

1= Yellow   2=Brown   3=Blue   4= Green

5=Pink   6=Purple   7=Red   8=Orange

1= Yellow   2=Brown   3=Blue   4= Green

5=Pink   6=Purple   7=Red   8=Orange

1= Yellow   2=Brown   3=Blue   4= Green

5=Pink   6=Purple   7=Orange   8=Red

1= Yellow 2=Brown 3=Blue 4= Pink

5=Purple 6=Red 7=Orange

1= Yellow   2=Brown   3=Blue   4= Green

5=Pink   6=Purple   7=Red   8=Orange

1= Yellow 2=Brown 3=Blue 4= Green

5=Pink 6=Purple 7=Red 8=Orange

1= Yellow   2=Brown   3=Blue   4= Green

5=Pink   6=Purple   7=Red   8=Orange

1= Yellow   2=Brown   3=Blue   4= Green
5=Pink   6=Purple   7=Red   8=Orange

1= Yellow   2=Brown   3=Blue   4= Green

5=Pink   6=Purple   7=Orange   8=Red

1= Yellow   2=Brown   3=Blue   4= Green

5=Pink   6=Purple   7=Red   8=Orange

1= Yellow   2=Brown   3=Blue   4= Green

5=Pink   6=Purple   7=Red   8=Orange

1= Yellow 2=Brown 3=Blue 4= Green

5=Pink 6=Purple 7=Red 8=Orange

1= Yellow   2=Orange   3=Blue   4= Green

5=Pink   6=Purple   7=Red

Thank you for purchasing the book. I hope you and your family members enjoyed coloring the pages.

Kindly **leave ratings and feedback** on Amazon so that it will help other people in deciding to purchase my books. I'll be very thankful to you.

If you want to write any personal note, feel free to send email at **sachin@sachinsachdev.com**

I respond to all the emails I receive.

Thank you
Sachin Sachdeva
Author and Illustrator

You might also like these Color By Number Books.

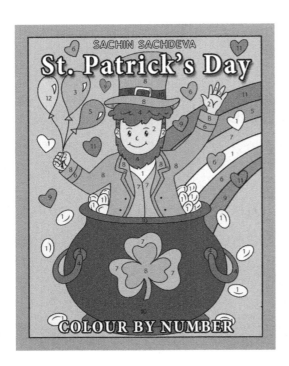

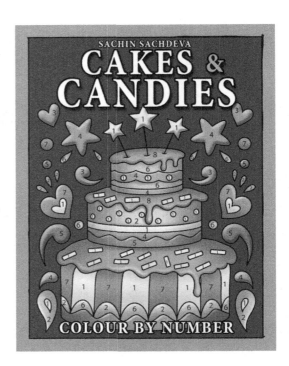

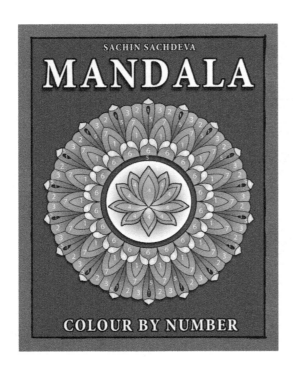

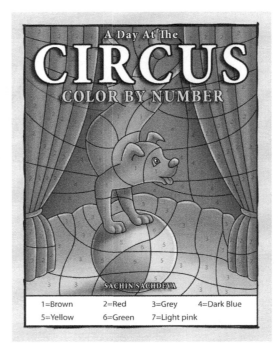

You might also like these Color By Number Books.

ISBN: 9781075372476

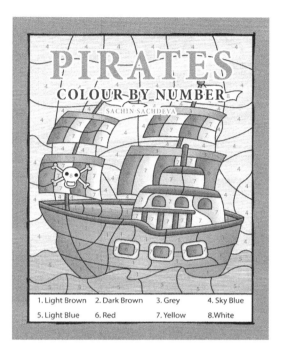

ISBN: 9781718941700

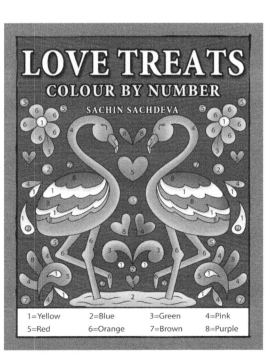

ISBN: 9781654940065

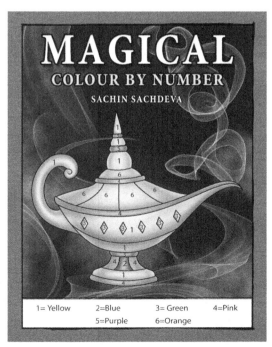

ISBN: 9781099409516

Join my Facebook Group for Freebies,
New Book launches and all the other updates.

Search for "Books by Sachin Sachdeva" on Facebook

I am also giving away Free 32 Coloring Pages PDF

 https://tinyurl.com/yx4483nj

I have includes few bonus pages from
"St. Patrick's Day" & "Dress Up" book.
Hope you enjoy coloring them too!

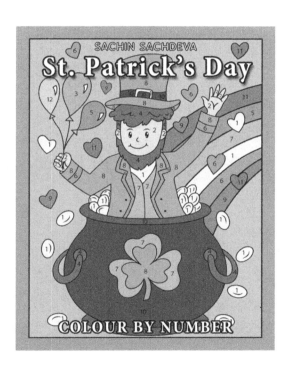

1 = Yellow	2 = Peach	3 = Pink	4 = Brown
5 = Blue	6 = Orange	7 = Lt. Green	8 = Green
9 = Red	10 = Black	11 = Purple	12 = Lt. Blue

1 = Yellow	2 = Peach	3 = Pink	4 = Brown
5 = Blue	6 = Orange	7 = Lt. Green	8 = Green
9 = Red	10 = Black	11 = Purple	12 = Lt. Blue

1 = Yellow	2 = Peach	3 = Pink	4 = Brown
5 = Blue	6 = Orange	7 = Lt. Green	8 = Green
9 = Red	10 = Black	11 = Purple	12 = Lt. Blue

1= Yellow   2=Blue   3= Green   4=Pink

5=Purple   6=Orange   7=Red   8=Brown

1= Yellow   2=Blue   3= Green   4=Pink

5=Purple   6=Orange   7=Red   8=Brown

1= Yellow   2=Blue   3= Green   4=Pink
5=Purple   6=Orange   7=Red   8=Brown

Made in the USA
Las Vegas, NV
21 December 2022

63835659R00037